GEORGE
and the
WHOPPER

Chris McTrustry

Illustrated by John Boucher

Rigby

Contents

CHAPTER 1

"Vegetables! Yuck!"

Dinnertime was not George's favorite meal of the day.

It used to be.

Hamburgers and fries, steak and fries, hot dogs and fries, chicken and fries. All yummy. All his favorites.

At least they used to be.

One night at the dinner table, Mom said, "George, you're getting older. You eat too many fries. It's time you started eating vegetables."

George hated vegetables.

"Try them," said Dad.

He put a big spoonful of vegetables onto George's plate.

But George clamped his mouth tight. He shook his head. No way was he eating that yucky green stuff.

"Vegetables are very good for you," said Mom, "and very tasty."

George unclamped his mouth. "They don't look good. And I'm sure they don't taste good either," he said. And again he clamped his mouth shut tight.

There was a knock at the back door. George's best friend, Lance E. Lott, walked inside.

"Hello, everyone," said Lance.

"Hello, Lance," said Mom.

"Hello, Lance," said Dad.

"Mmmm-o, mmmm-nce," said George.

Lance gave George a funny look. That was the strangest "Hello, Lance" he had ever heard. "Is George ready to go to the movies?" asked Lance.

George unclamped his mouth. "Yes!" he cried.

"No, he is not," said Dad.

"He refuses to eat his vegetables," Mom explained to Lance.

"And he is not going anywhere until he eats them," said Dad.

CHAPTER 2

BIG Trouble

"Vegetables are yucky," said George. He clamped his mouth shut. Five minutes passed. Ten minutes passed.

Finally, Dad stood up and went over to the telephone. "You leave me no choice," he said and started to dial. He sounded very, very serious.

"Hello, I would like to speak to the President, please," Dad said into the phone.

The President?

The leader of the country!

Lance tugged on George's sleeve and asked, "Why is your dad calling the President?"

"I don't know," said George.

Dad put his hand over the phone. "If George won't eat his vegetables when we ask him," said Dad, "maybe he will when the President asks him."

"Wow!" said Lance.

"Oh no," thought George. He was in BIG trouble.

CHAPTER 3

BIGGER Trouble

Dad spoke to the President for a few minutes. Most of the time he said, "I see," and "That would be wonderful."

George and Lance watched and listened.

Finally, Dad said "goodbye" and put down the phone. "The President is a very busy man," he said. "But he is coming here on Thursday night."

The next morning, George met up with Lance E. Lott outside his house. They walked down the sidewalk, heading for the school bus stop at the corner.

Mrs. Crabapple waved to the boys from her front yard. Mrs. Crabapple was a widow and one of George's best friends.

"Good morning, George. Good morning, Lance," said Mrs. Crabapple.

"Hi," mumbled George.

"Hello, Mrs. Crabapple," said Lance.

Mrs. Crabapple stopped watering her flowers.

"What's the matter, George?" said Mrs. Crabapple. "You look like you lost a dollar and picked up a dime."

"The President is coming to visit George on Thursday night," said Lance.

Down the road, the school bus chugged toward the bus stop.

"There's the bus, Lance!" cried George.

"We better hurry or we'll miss it and be late for school," said Lance.

They started to run down the sidewalk.

"Why is the President coming to see George?" Mrs. Crabapple called after them. This was BIG news.

"Because of my vegetables," George yelled over his shoulder to Mrs. Crabapple.

Mrs. Crabapple stroked her wrinkly chin.

"Well," thought Mrs. Crabapple, "a visit from the President to honor vegetables grown by George!" Her friends at the garden club would love to hear this news.

CHAPTER 4

Gossip Travels

Mrs. Crabapple's garden club friends were *very* impressed when they heard about the President's visit.

"My husband hasn't said anything about a visit," sniffed the Mayor's wife. "And he *is* the Mayor."

"George told me himself," said Mrs. Crabapple. "The President will be here on Thursday night."

When the garden club meeting was over, the Mayor's wife hurried to her car. She drove to city hall and told her husband, the Mayor, about the President's visit.

"The President will be visiting town on Thursday," she told her husband, the Mayor. "Young George's vegetables are the best in town. He is going to receive an award."

After his wife left, the Mayor called the state's Senator.

"The President will be visiting town on Thursday," the Mayor told the Senator. "Young George's vegetables are the best in the state. He is going to receive a big award."

"The President hasn't told me about this award," said the Senator. "I will check with the White House."

The Senator called the White House. She spoke to the President's assistant.

"The President will be visiting a town in our state on Thursday," the Senator told the assistant. "Young George's vegetables are the best in the country. He is going to receive a huge award."

The assistant carefully checked the President's list of places to visit and people to see.

George was not on the list.

The President's assistant scratched his head. "I will talk to the President," the assistant told the Senator.

CHAPTER 5

A Surprise Visitor

*T*hat night, George still refused to eat his vegetables.

"You had better eat your vegetables, George," said Mom. "Don't forget who is coming on Thursday." Mom winked at Dad and smiled.

George shook his head and clamped his mouth tight.

"Something strange happened to-day," said Dad. "The Mayor came up to me and shook my hand."

"Why?" asked Mom.

"I haven't got a clue," said Dad. "He said we must be very proud."

"Of what?" asked Mom.

"I haven't got a clue," said Dad.

"Very strange," said Mom.

"Yes," said Dad. "Very strange."

George said nothing. He kept his mouth clamped shut.

On Thursday night, George still refused to eat his vegetables.

"I thought the President was coming to speak to me," laughed George.

"Go to your room," said Dad. "Right now!"

George went to his room. He flopped down on his bed. He was very hungry. But no matter how hungry he was, no vegetables would ever pass through his lips. Never, ever.

Suddenly, there was a lot of cheering and shouting outside. George pulled the curtains back and peeped down into the street.

The street outside his house was jam-packed. Row after row of TV reporters stood in front of row after row of TV cameras. And the rows of TV reporters and the rows of TV cameras were all pointed at George's house.

A big, black car glided to a stop in front of the house. A man in a dark suit rushed forward and opened the back door of the car.

A man climbed out of the car. He was tall and had a big droopy moustache.

George knew who that man was. The President!

CHAPTER 6

"No Vegetables For Me, Either!"

Mom and Dad could not believe it. The President and the First Lady were sitting in their living room. The President and the First Lady—sitting on their couch!

"I am here to present an award to George," the President told Mom and Dad.

"What's the award for?" asked Mom.

"The award is for growing the finest vegetables in the country," said the President.

Mom and Dad looked at each other. They didn't know what to say. Finally, Dad said, "But George doesn't grow vegetables."

"Very strange," said the President.

"How did you find out about George and the vegetables?" asked Mom.

"My assistant told me," said the President. "The state Senator told him. The Mayor told the Senator. The Mayor's wife told the Mayor. And, I believe, a lady from town, Mrs. Crabapple, told the Mayor's wife."

"Who told Mrs. Crabapple?" asked a very puzzled Dad.

"I did," said George. George walked into the room and shook the President's hand.

"Are you here to make me eat my vegetables?" asked George.

Dad explained to the President how he had pretended to call him. "I thought it might make George eat his vegetables," said Dad.

"And did you?" the President asked George.

"No way," said George. And he clamped his mouth tight.

"Good for you," the President said. "I don't like vegetables either."

Mom placed a plate of vegetables on the table in front of George. And a plate in front of the President.

"Are you both going to eat your vegetables?" asked Mom.

"No way," said George. And he clamped his mouth tight.

"No way," said the President. And he clamped his mouth tight, too.

"You are a very bad President," said the First Lady.

Mom and Dad and the First Lady went into the kitchen.

CHAPTER 7

"Vegetables Are Good"

George tapped the President on the arm. "Are you going to eat your vegetables?" he asked.

The President shook his head. "I am the leader of the country," he said. "I don't have to eat vegetables if I don't want to."

The President looked toward the kitchen. "And I don't want to!" he called out.

George looked at the plate of vegetables sitting in front of him. Maybe Dad and Mom were right. Maybe vegetables WERE very good for him. And very tasty.

"I think we should try the vegetables," George said softly.

"What?" howled the President. "Never!"

George looked up at the President. He took a deep breath. "But if you don't eat your vegetables, no one will," said George.

"What do you mean?" asked the President.

George pointed out the window. There were even more TV trucks outside his house now. "The whole country must be watching," he thought.

"If all the kids find out you refuse to eat your vegetables, they might not eat their vegetables either," said George.

"Well, good for them," said the President.

"But what about the people who grow the vegetables? And the people who sell them? They won't have any jobs," said George. "And Mom and Dad said vegetables are good for you—tasty and healthy."

The President stroked his chin and nodded.

"So we have to eat our vegetables for our own good. And for the good of the country," he said.

"Yes," said George, "we have to."

"Very well," said the President.

He turned toward the kitchen and called out, "We'll eat our vegetables!" Mom and Dad and the First Lady hurried out and cheered.

The President winked at Mom and Dad and said, "George has taught me a valuable lesson today."

"That's right," said George. "Don't be afraid to try something new."

George winked at Mom and Dad and smiled.